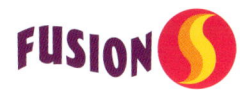

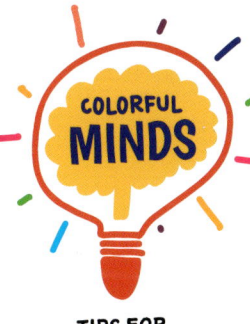

COLORFUL MINDS

TIPS FOR MANAGING YOUR EMOTIONS

FUSION

The Red Book

What to Do When You're Angry

by
William Anthony

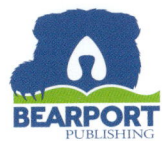

BEARPORT PUBLISHING

Minneapolis, Minnesota

Credits

Cover and throughout -Ekaterina Kapranova, Beatriz Gascon J. 4 - NLshop. 6 - xpixel. 7 - My Portfolio, Nikolaeva. 8 - studiovin. 11 - Kay Cee Lens and Footages. 13 - Diego Schtutman. 15 - grmarc, Nadezda Barkova, pxhidalgo, andyKRAKOVSKI. 16 - Team Ok-topus, Andriy Blokhin. 18 - Africa Studio 22 - NLshop. Additional illustrations by Danielle Webster-Jones. All images courtesy of shutterstock.com. With thanks to Getty Images, Thinkstock Photo and iStockphoto.

Library of Congress Cataloging-in-Publication Data is available at www.loc.gov or upon request from the publisher.

ISBN: 978-1-64747-580-2 (hardcover)
ISBN: 978-1-64747-585-7 (paperback)
ISBN: 978-1-64747-590-1 (ebook)

© 2022 Booklife Publishing

This edition is published by arrangement with Booklife Publishing.

North American adaptations ©2022 Bearport Publishing Company. All rights reserved. No part of this publication may be reproduced in whole or in part, stored in any retrieval system, or transmitted in any form or by any means, electronic, mechanical, photocopying, recording, or otherwise, without written permission from the publisher.

For more information, write to Bearport Publishing, 5357 Penn Avenue South, Minneapolis, MN 55419. Printed in the United States of America.

For more The Red Book activities:

1. Go to **www.factsurfer.com**

2. Enter "**Red Book**" into the search box.

3. Click on the cover of this book to see a list of activities.

CONTENTS

Imagine a Rainbow 4
Target Practice 6
The Shout Hole 8
Clear Your Mind.................... 10
Push the Buttons................... 12
I'm So Angry, I Could 14
The Calm Elevator 16
Super You......................... 18
Little Ideas........................ 20
Feeling Better?..................... 22
Glossary 24
Index 24

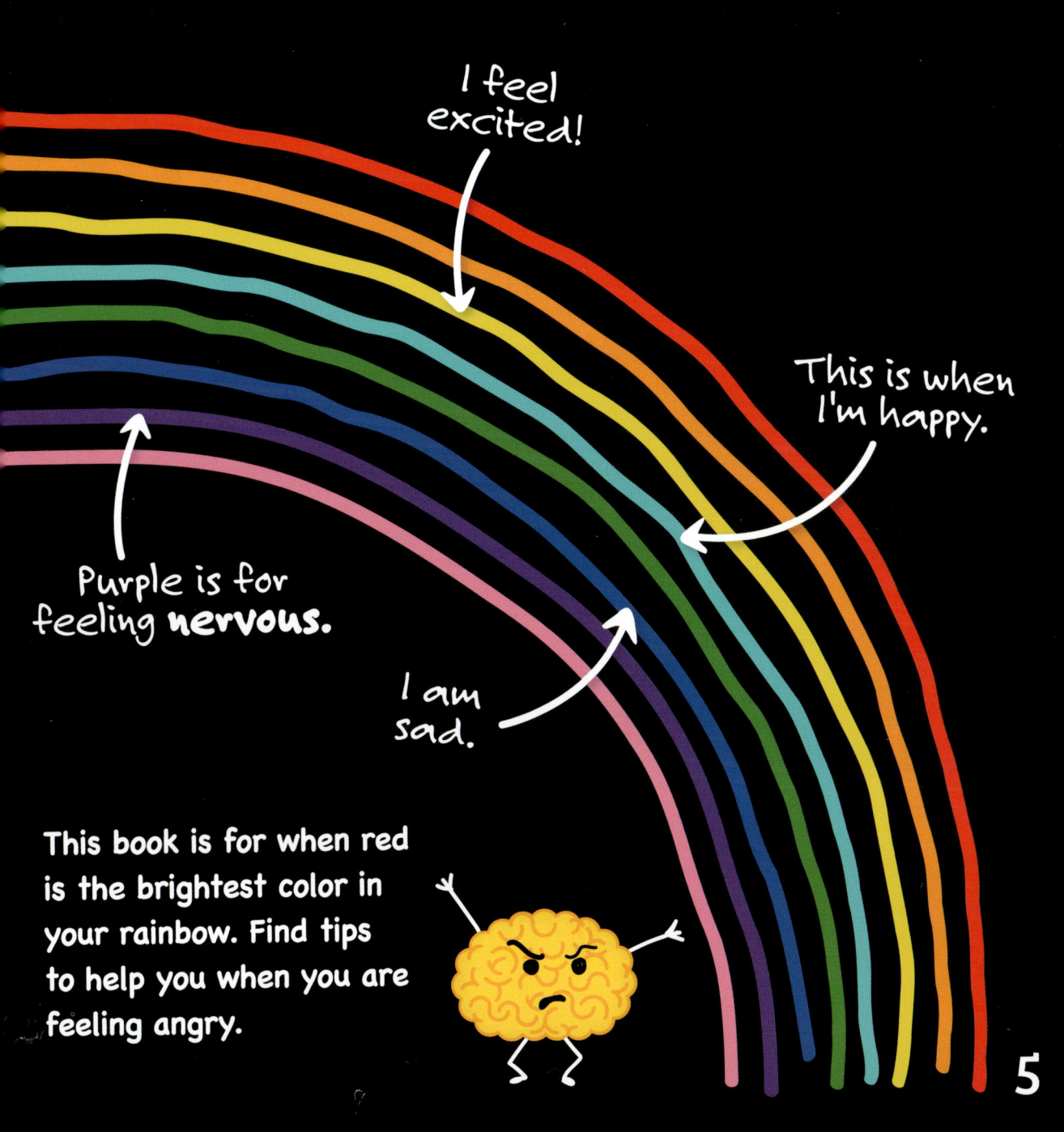

TARGET PRACTICE

When we are angry, we might shout and scream or throw things around. But that's not good for anyone.

> If you feel the need to throw something, you can safely aim at this **target**.

Lean this book against something. Grab some scrap paper and scrunch it up into a ball. Take a few steps back and throw the paper ball at the target as hard as you can!

TOP TIP!
Make sure you have lots of space around you so you don't bump into anything.

THROW PAPER AT THIS!

AIM HERE!

THE SHOUT HOLE

Have you ever been so angry that you just wanted to shout at the person or thing that was making you mad?

We think that screaming at someone will make us feel better. But it doesn't help, and it can make things worse.

Meet the shout hole. You can shout whatever you want into it!

TOP TIP!
Take the shout hole to a quiet room away from other people so you can be as loud as you need to be.

THE SHOUT HOLE

SHOUT HERE!

CLEAR YOUR MIND

It's hard to think clearly or make good decisions when you are angry. Some people say that anger makes their mind feel cloudy.

If your mind is feeling cloudy, try this.

Lie on your back somewhere comfortable and hold this book above your head. Take a deep breath, and then slowly try to blow the clouds away!

TOP TIP! When you don't have this book with you, you can close your eyes and imagine the clouds instead.

10

Take a deep breath.
This is a big one!

A long, slow breath might move this one!

Blow this one away!

11

PUSH THE BUTTONS

Exercise makes our bodies and our minds feel better. So let's get moving and get happy!

> Find an open area with nothing to bump into and stand this book up. There are five buttons on the next page that you need to press in order.

To get a good **workout**, you must choose a place far away from the book that you need to run to before you press the next button!

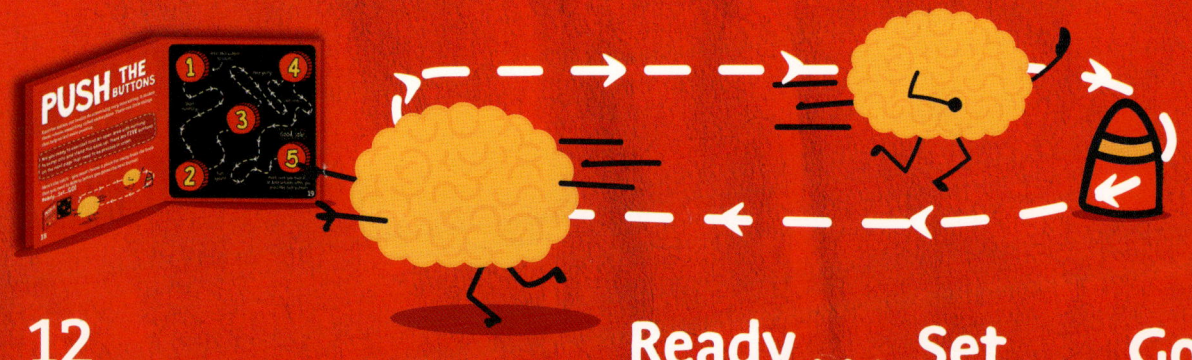

Ready... Set... Go!

I'M SO ANGRY, I COULD

A good way to deal with anger is to talk about what's bothering you. But sometimes, this seems too hard to do.

It's okay if talking about your feelings out loud seems too scary. Instead, you can write your feelings.

Cut or tear a sheet of paper into four pieces. On each one, write:

"I'm so angry, I could . . ."

Then, finish the sentence and draw a picture.

TOP TIP! Instead of saying it out loud, you can show your drawings to a trusted adult to let them know how you feel.

Here are some examples:

I'm so angry, I could explode like a volcano!

I'm so angry, I could **wrestle** a hippo!

I'm so angry, I could pop a million balloons!

I'm so angry, I could shout loud enough to start an earthquake!

15

THE CALM ELEVATOR

When we are angry, we breathe quickly. Breathing slowly can help us **relax**.

Imagine you are a tall building. Sit or stand up straight and place one hand on top of the other one and near your waist.

Your bottom hand is the ground floor, and your top hand is an **elevator**. As you breathe in, raise the elevator hand up. As you breathe out, bring it back down.

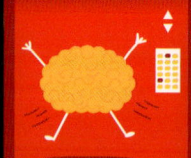

BREATHING IN

Move your elevator up slowly as you breathe in.

BREATHING OUT

Move your elevator down slowly as you breathe out.

SUPER-YOU

Sometimes we might shout at someone when we don't mean to. Then, when we've calmed down, we might feel bad about it. This is okay!

> When we feel like this, it is important to remember how super we are!

Get a trusted adult or friend and follow the steps on the next page together.

STEP 1:
Get some pencils and paper.

STEP 2:
Write or draw something you are good at or why people like you. Don't let the other person see!

STEP 3:
At the same time, ask the other person to do the same thing about you. Don't look at their paper either!

STEP 4:
When you are both finished, show each other what makes you so super!

LITTLE IDEAS

There are lots of little tips and tricks you can use when you feel angry.

COUNT DOWN

Count down from 10 if you're feeling angry. It will make you feel calmer.

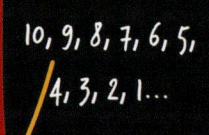

YOUR HAPPY PLACE

Find somewhere quiet, and close your eyes. Imagine a **peaceful**, relaxing place. What color is the sky? What can you see? What can you hear?

TALKING TIMER

When we are angry, we might say something we don't mean. Give yourself a few seconds before talking. This will help you speak in a calmer and nicer way.

STRETCH

Gently rolling your neck and your shoulders can help relax your mind and body.

SWEET DREAMS

Make sure you get enough sleep every night. This will help you feel better and happier.

FEELING BETTER?

Which tip worked best for you? Why do you think that is?

If you feel calmer, now is a good time to think about what made you feel angry and why. How might you handle things the next time you feel angry?

Remember, you are like everyone else. We all have colorful minds.

Every feeling you have is important! This book will still be here

whenever

you need it.

GLOSSARY

elevator a machine used to carry people and things to different floors in a building

exercise movements you make to become stronger and healthier

nervous worried or afraid about what might happen

peaceful quiet and calm

relax to stop feeling nervous or worried

target a mark you try to hit with a tossed object, such as a beanbag or crumpled piece of paper

workout an activity or exercise that improves your health and makes you stronger

wrestle to struggle or fight with someone or something

INDEX

breathing 10–11, 13, 16–17
calm 16, 18, 20–22
exercise 12
imagination 4, 10, 16, 20

relaxing 16, 20–21
shouting 6, 8–9, 15, 18
sleep 21
talking 14, 21